A Birthday Present for Piglet

A
MOUSE WORKS
MAKE BELIEVE
STORYBOOK

One fine morning, Winnie the Pooh thought happily, "Today is Piglet's birthday party! I think I'll give him honey."

So he got a special birthday box and poured the honey in, but it poured right out again.

"Oh bother!" said Pooh. "I'd better ask Rabbit what to do!"

"Rabbit!" called Pooh. "It's Piglet's birthday and I have a birthday box, but nothing to put in it."

"Carrots," said Rabbit importantly. "Let's fill the box with carrots."

The two set to work, getting so excited they picked a whole row of carrots.

"Oh, gracious!" said Pooh. "There are too many carrots for the box."

Rabbit considered the matter and said, "How about a carrot cake for the party?"

"Hurrah!" said Pooh. "That will be scrumdelicious. But what will I put in the birthday box?"

Pooh worried and wandered until he met Tigger and Roo, who were out in the woods practicing bouncing.

"Tigger and Roo," called Pooh, "what can I put inside Piglet's birthday box?"

"I know!" said Roo. He bounced home and came back with a big red balloon.

"Your present is very nice, and the string's a perfect fit," said Pooh to Roo.

"But," said Eeyore joining the friends, "in a blustery wind the balloon will make the birthday box float away."

"Then Tigger will bounce up and get it," said you-know-who.

"But it will be Piglet's balloon, Tigger," Pooh pointed out. "And Piglets don't bounce."

"Aw, no," sighed Tigger. "I guess the balloon can't go in the birthday box."

"It can still go to the party," said Roo. "It can decorate the table."

"That's wonderful," said Pooh. "But all I have to bring is—"

"The birthday box," said Eeyore.

"With nothing in it," said Pooh sadly.

"It's the thought that counts," said Roo.

"I have an idea, but it probably won't work," said Eeyore, taking the box from Pooh. "Meet me at the party."

So that afternoon, all the friends
gathered around to celebrate Piglet's
birthday. Everyone was there—everyone
that is except Eeyore, which made Pooh
feel pretty worried.

"What a w-w-wonderful party," said
Piglet, "with hats and balloons and a cake."

Pooh tried to sound cheerful as he said, "Rabbit made the cake, and Roo brought the decorations, and I...well, I..."

"Brought the birthday present," said Eeyore arriving at last.

"Whatever can be in it?" wondered Piglet.

Pooh wondered, too.

What was in it was Eeyore's tail. He had brought it just for the afternoon so everyone could play "Pin-the-Tail-on-the-Donkey."

"That's the best birthday present I've ever gotten... I mean given," said Pooh, hugging Eeyore.